ASTRID & APOLLO

AND THE
FAMILY FUN FAIR DAY

BY
V.T. BIDANIA

ILLUSTRATED BY
EVELT YANAIT

PICTUF

To Trystan & Justyn—VTB

Published by Picture Window Books,
an imprint of Capstone.
1710 Roe Crest Drive
North Mankato, Minnesota 56003
capstonepub.com

Library of Congress Cataloging-in-Publication Data is available on the Library of
Congress website.
ISBN: 9781666337464 (hardcover)
ISBN: 9781666337426 (paperback)
ISBN: 9781666337389 (ebook PDF)

Summary: It's time for the fair! Astrid, Apollo, Eliana, and their parents head
out for a day of fun, food, and family. The fair is hosting a scavenger hunt, and
they join the game to find mystery items based on the five senses. But the biggest
puzzle of all is trying to figure out what Eliana is asking for! As they hunt their
way through the list, eating their favorite foods and playing their favorite games,
will they finally discover what Eliana's favorite is?

Designer: Tracy Davies

Design Elements: Shutterstock/Ingo Menhard, 60, Shutterstock/Yangxiong
(Hmong pattern), 5 and throughout

Printed and bound in the USA. 4882

Table of Contents

Hi, I'm Astrid. My twin brother is Apollo, and we were born in Minnesota. We live here with our mom, dad, and little sister, Eliana.

ASTRID GAO NOU

Hi, I'm Apollo! Our mom and dad were both born in Laos. They came to the United States when they were very young and grew up here.

APOLLO NOU KOU

MOM, DAD, AND ELIANA GAO CHEE

HMONG WORDS

gao (GOW)—girl; it is often placed in front of a girl's name. Hmong spelling: *nkauj*

Gao Chee (GOW chee)—shiny girl. Hmong spelling: *Nkauj Ci*

Gao Hlee (GOW lee)—moon girl. Hmong spelling: *Nkauj Hli*

Gao Nou (GOW new)—sun girl. Hmong spelling: *Nkauj Hnub*

Hmong (MONG)—a group of people who came to the U.S. from Laos. Many Hmong from Laos now live in Minnesota. Hmong spelling: *Hmoob*

Nia Thy (nee-YAH thy)—grandmother on the mother's side. Hmong spelling: *Niam Tais*

Nou Kou (NEW koo)—star. Hmong spelling: *Hnub Qub*

tou (TOO)—boy or son; it is often placed in front of a boy's name. Hmong spelling: *tub*

CHAPTER 1

Family Fun Fair Day

Astrid and Apollo stepped off the bus. They looked around the big parking lot.

"We're here!" said Astrid.

"It's going to be so fun!" said Apollo.

More buses were driving into the lot. Groups of people were walking toward the main entrance. Up ahead, the giant Ferris wheel filled the sky.

Astrid and Apollo smiled at each other. They were so excited to be at the annual state fair.

They never got tired of the rides, the games, the animals, or the exhibits. Most of all, they loved the food.

"People! People!" said Eliana, pointing at the crowds lining up.

"Yes, lots of people. Lots of lines too," said Dad. He lifted Eliana onto his shoulders.

"Good thing we already have our tickets. We won't have to wait in a long line to buy them," Mom said.

"Stay together, everybody!" said Dad.

The twins followed their parents and Eliana through the gate. They could smell the corn dogs and cotton candy in the air.

They saw colorful gondola cars moving along the cables high overhead. A little boy inside a red car waved down at them.

They were still waving back when a teenage girl walked up to them.

"Welcome! Would you like to go on a scavenger hunt?" the girl asked them.

"What kind of scavenger hunt?" asked Dad.

"For Family Fun Fair Day!" she said.

"How do we play?" asked Astrid.

The girl handed them a pencil and a piece of green paper that had nine squares on it.

"Go around the fair. Use your five senses to look for things listed in these boxes. When you find something that matches, write it in the box," she explained.

"Our five senses?" Apollo said.

"Yes! You'll want to search for things you can see, hear, touch, smell, and taste. Once you have filled in each box, turn in your sheet, and you'll win a prize!"

Eliana looked at her with a curious face.

"Prize?" she said.

"What's the prize?" Astrid and Apollo asked at the same time.

"The prize is a *surprise*! But I think you'll like it," the girl said.

She pointed to the map on the back of the paper. "Come here to this *X* to collect your prize when you're done. Good luck!"

She gave them a big smile and walked over to another family.

Astrid looked at the sheet. There were nine squares with different words written in each. One square had the word *hot*. Another had the word *cold*. In other squares, she saw *loud, sour, sweet,* and other words.

"Can we play?" Astrid asked her parents. She loved scavenger hunts—she was really good at finding things!

"We could win the surprise prize! Whatever that is," Apollo said with a laugh.

Mom nodded. "A scavenger hunt at the fair will make the day even more fun."

"What a good idea to use your five senses," said Dad. "I'll be in charge of all the tasting ones!" he joked.

"Yay!" said Astrid.

Apollo looked down at Eliana.

"Do you want to go on the scavenger hunt too?" he asked her.

Eliana shook her head and shouted, "No! Soo-per sip-puh-dee!" as she did a little dance.

"Please stop shouting, Eliana," Mom said and patted Eliana's head.

They walked down the main street of the fair.

They passed other families waiting to buy foot-long hot dogs, buckets of french fries, and giant bags of caramel popcorn.

"Astrid, can I see the paper, please?" Mom asked.

They stopped while she read it over.

"Why don't we find the easy things first? Here it says *cold*. Let's start with that," Mom said.

"I'm thirsty, so how about a cold drink?" Dad suggested.

"I want something cold too," said Apollo. He pointed to a drink stand. "Over there!"

They got in line and Dad ordered an ice-cold soda for himself.

Everyone else ordered snow cones—lime, cherry, blueberry, and mango!

"Brrr!" Astrid said after she took her first bite. She looked at the scavenger hunt sheet and wrote *icy soda* and *snow cones* in the *cold* box. "One down, eight to go! What should we hunt for next?"

"Soo-per sip-puh-dee!" Eliana yelled around a mouthful of cherry snow cone.

"Super sip? Dad, I think she wants a sip of your soda," Apollo said.

"No sip!" Eliana shouted.

"Eliana, you're being too loud again," said Astrid.

Eliana stuck out her bottom lip.

Apollo saw the box that said *colorful*. "Let's find something we can look at. There are colors all around us—which should we choose for the scavenger hunt?"

Just as he said that, Astrid noticed a big sign right above Apollo's head. It read "The Big and Beautiful Butterfly Forest."

"We can go in there to look at colorful butterflies!" she said.

CHAPTER 2

Butterflies and Music

The Big and Beautiful Butterfly Forest was inside a building with a high ceiling. It was filled with trees and flowers. Butterflies of every color fluttered around.

Mom and Dad took pictures as a playful yellow butterfly perched on Astrid's shoulder.

A blue butterfly landed on Apollo's head. He tried to look up at it, but he couldn't see it. "Is it still there? Did it fly away yet?" he asked, holding still so he wouldn't scare it away.

Astrid giggled. "It isn't moving. Maybe it fell asleep!"

An orange butterfly flew onto Eliana's shirtsleeve. Then a blue one landed on her arm, and a brown one perched on her hand. It had big circles on its wings that looked like eyes!

Eliana stared at the brown butterfly's wings. They gently fluttered up and down.

"Look! Look!" she said.

Mom took more pictures as people gathered around to see all the butterflies on Eliana.

"They must think Eliana is a flower!" Dad said. "A beautiful flower for beautiful butterflies."

Mom nodded. "Yes, beautiful! And now we can check *colorful* off the list!"

* * *

They left the Big and Beautiful Butterfly Forest and headed over to the midway—the part of the fair with the rides!

Huge roller coasters rose high into the sky. The spaceship ride spun around and around in a circle. People climbed into the giant slingshot ride, ready to be tossed into the air.

"Scary!" Eliana said, her eyes big.

Astrid agreed. "I don't want to ride that ever!"

"I do!" said Apollo, laughing. "Or maybe next year. . . ."

Then they heard music coming from the grandstand—the big stage where bands and performers put on shows.

"Is that a concert?" Mom asked.

Dad read the grandstand sign and said, "The International Hmong Day program is starting now. Let's go see the celebration!"

"Sip-puh-dee?" Eliana said, but everyone else was too busy trying to hear the music to notice.

* * *

Astrid and Apollo sat with their family and watched the grandstand stage. A Hmong band played a happy song. The audience clapped along to the guitars, keyboard, and drums.

Next a Hmong dance troupe performed a lively dance. The silver coins from their costumes jingled as the performers danced to loud music. They did flips and leaps and spins! Everyone cheered.

Then a singer came on to the stage wearing a bright, shiny Hmong dress. She sang a pretty song that made everyone smile.

Afterward, a man with a microphone thanked everyone for celebrating International Hmong Day.

As Astrid and Apollo walked out of the grandstand, they talked excitedly.

"I'm glad we saw that!" said Apollo.

"Me too! Thanks for taking us, Dad," said Astrid.

"It was a really nice show," Mom agreed.

"We heard great music in there too," said Astrid.

"Yes, *loud* music!" Apollo said and looked at the scavenger hunt sheet. "Now we can cross off the *loud* box!"

Eliana pulled at the sheet in Apollo's hand. She said, "Sip-puh-dee! NOW!"

"Eliana, please give back the sheet," said Apollo. "Let's see what's next on our scavenger hunt!"

Eliana squeezed her eyes shut and made fists at her sides.

Astrid saw the word *hot* on the sheet and said, "Can we look for something hot?"

"Let's see . . . " said Apollo, thinking. He looked around and spotted corn husks stacked high in a garbage can. People stood nearby eating corn. "How about corn on the cob?" Apollo said.

Astrid glanced over at the booth selling corn. "They're hot from being on the grill."

"They're yummy too," said Mom.

"Let's get some!" said Dad.

As they stood in line, Astrid and Apollo watched the crowds of people at the fair. They saw a group of kids walk by carrying the green scavenger hunt sheet.

"That was a cool prize!" one of them said, smiling. The others nodded.

"The coolest!" another kid said.

Astrid and Apollo grinned at each other.

"I really wonder what the prize could be," said Apollo.

"We're going to find out!" said Astrid.

When it was their turn, Mom bought five cobs of corn. Melted butter dripped down the sides. The corn felt warm in their hands.

Astrid and Apollo sat on the grass. Mom, Dad, and Eliana sat on a bench nearby.

"These are so good!" said Astrid, wiping her buttery chin with a napkin.

Apollo nodded. "Just as good as the corn from Nia Thy's farm."

Eliana took a bite and nodded.

Apollo wiped the butter off his fingers, then crossed out *hot* on the green sheet. He read the remaining boxes. "Next we need to find something *wet or slippery*. Where can we find that?"

Eliana squealed, "Sip-puh-dee! Over there!"

"Why do you keep saying that?" Astrid asked.

Eliana jumped up and pointed in the distance. But instead of what Eliana was pointing at, Astrid saw the aquarium. Its entrance was just past where Eliana stood.

The aquarium had a big picture of stingrays hanging in the window.

Above the picture, a sign read, "Pet real stingrays!"

"Stingrays are in water, which is wet! Eliana, you found the perfect thing for us!" said Astrid.

CHAPTER 3

Stingrays and Smelly Smells

"Can we go to the aquarium?" Apollo asked Mom and Dad.

Mom and Dad nodded, and Eliana chased after the twins as they went inside.

In the aquarium, kids were lining up next to a long tank. Small stingrays swam around in it. Workers stood by to answer questions about the different kinds of stingrays.

"Does it hurt if you touch them?" asked Astrid.

"These stingrays won't hurt you, but you do have to be gentle," said the worker. He showed them how to hold out their hands. "Be very careful when you touch the top of the stingray."

Astrid, Apollo, and Eliana watched the stingrays glide by. It looked like they were flying through the water!

"The skin looks so smooth," said Astrid.

"It soft?" asked Eliana.

"I'll go first and let you know," said Apollo. He lowered his hand into the water. The stingray swam under his hand, then paused. Apollo slowly wiggled his fingers.

"It's not slippery—it's rough," said Apollo. "It feels sandy!"

Astrid petted another stingray and said, "Like sandpaper!"

Then it was Eliana's turn. She giggled when the stingray swam under her hand.

When they were done petting the stingrays, Apollo looked at the sheet again. "We're all done with touch, hear, and see!"

"Now we just need smell and taste," Astrid said, looking over Apollo's shoulder at the sheet.

As Astrid and Apollo walked outside, a breeze blew by. A smell hit their noses. But it didn't smell like the yummy food smells of the fair.

Astrid wrinkled her nose. "It smells like a farm!" she said.

Eliana pinched her nose with her fingers. Dad smiled and copied her.

Apollo turned to see where the smell was coming from. "It's the barn!"

"Let's go visit the animals!" said Astrid.

"Is there a box on the sheet that says stinky?" Mom asked with a laugh.

"There is one that says *strong smell*. And this is a really *smelly* smell! I think that counts!" said Apollo.

Eliana pointed in the direction opposite the barn. "No, go sip-puh-dee!"

Dad picked her up and asked, "Don't you want to pet the animals?"

Eliana pouted and flopped in Dad's arms.

Inside the barn, families lined up to see farm animals. One section of the barn had pink pigs, brown pigs, and little spotted piglets. Another section had fluffy white sheep and noisy gray goats.

On the other side of the barn were black and white cows and brown cows. One little calf wobbled up close to the gate. It looked up at Astrid and Apollo with big, dark eyes.

"That calf is so cute!" said Astrid.

"It would be neat to have as a pet!" said Apollo.

Then a man with a name tag that read Farmer Frank showed everyone how to milk a cow. He smiled at Eliana and said, "Would you like to try?"

But Eliana didn't want to. She hid her face in Dad's shirt.

When they were done looking at the sheep, goats, and pigs, the twins headed out of the barn with their family.

"That was fun. And the baby barn animals were so sweet. I want to take all of them home!" said Astrid.

"They were cute, but some of them were a little smelly. They can live in your room," Apollo joked.

"Lot smelly!" said Eliana. "Sooper sip-puh-dee now!"

CHAPTER 4

Game Time!

"What is she saying?" said Astrid.

"We don't understand you," Apollo said.

Eliana's cheeks turned red as she said, "Now, now, now!"

"Can you show us what you mean, Eliana?" Mom asked.

Eliana sat on the ground and threw her arms up. "Soo-per sip-puh-dee!"

Everyone looked at her, confused.

Dad picked her up. "Maybe a ride will cheer her up."

Eliana opened her mouth wide and cried, "Sip-puh-dee, sip-puh-dee, sip-puh-dee!"

"How about games? Maybe games will calm her down," Mom suggested.

"I'll play some games!" Astrid said. She loved the games at the fair, even if it was almost impossible to win the biggest prizes.

The games' flashing lights and colors were pretty to look at. It was fun hearing the workers calling out for people to play. When someone won a game, a loud bell clanged *ding-ding-ding!* and people cheered.

Mom gave them tickets to play games, and Astrid and Apollo took Eliana by the hands.

"Do you want to play pick-a-duck first? Or the fishing game?" asked Apollo.

Astrid smiled. She liked both of those games because players always won a prize. Even if the prizes were small, it was fun to play. She hoped that would cheer up Eliana.

Eliana was still grumpy, but she pointed at the pick-a-duck game.

Apollo handed the worker a ticket, and Eliana reached toward the ducks floating on the water. She caught one, looked at the letter under the duck, and showed the worker. He smiled and gave her a small, white toy dog.

"Fantastic job, Eliana!" said Dad.

Eliana hugged the little dog. Then she gave it to Astrid to put in her pocket to keep safe.

Apollo said, "Should we do the fishing game now?"

Eliana nodded.

Astrid and Apollo played the game with Eliana. They used short fishing poles to catch plastic fish from a small pool. A magnet on the fishing line connected with a piece of metal in the fish. Each fish had a number on it. When they caught their fish, they showed the numbers to the worker, and the worker handed them prizes.

"I won a stuffed fish!" Apollo cheered.

"And I won a unicorn!" said Astrid.

"What about you, Eliana?"

Eliana showed them her prize, which was a little purple octopus.

"That's cool, Eliana!" said Apollo.

"Want to trade?" Astrid asked her.

Eliana shook her head and smiled.

"At least she's smiling now," said Astrid.

Apollo nodded. "Are you happy now?" he asked Eliana.

Eliana shrugged and whispered, "Soo-per, soo-per."

The twins looked at each other and shrugged too.

As they walked by the ring toss game, the worker called into a megaphone.

"Step right up! Win a giant boat, a giant truck, or a giant snake! Toss one ring around a bottle, and pick your prize!"

Huge yellow, green, and blue plastic blow-up boats, trucks, and snakes hung above the glass bottles. The worker waved at Dad.

"Step right up. Give it a try!" he said.

Dad turned to look at the prizes and grinned.

"You've always wanted a boat," Mom teased him.

"Try it, Dad!" said Apollo.

"Do it, Dad! Win us a boat!" Astrid said.

The twins jumped up and down.

They were excited for Dad to play.

Eliana was excited too. "Boat, boat, boat!" she said.

* * *

Dad didn't win the giant boat. But the rings he threw landed very close to the bottles, so he won a tiny inflatable boat.

The kids walked away with their prizes. Dad handed Mom his boat.

"Just what I always wanted!" she said, and Dad smiled proudly.

Apollo held up his stuffed fish. "That was fun! And we're almost done with the scavenger hunt. We only have *taste* left."

"Which is good, because I'm hungry!" Astrid said.

"Well then, let's eat!" said Mom.

Astrid quickly checked the scavenger hunt sheet. "Let's eat and fill in the TASTE boxes. We need to get things that are *sweet, sour,* and *salty.*"

"I want the Large & Chubby Bacon Strips. Those are my favorite," said Dad.

"I'd like bacon too," said Mom.

Apollo nodded. "I want a Giant Turkey on a Stick!"

"Don't you mean drumstick?" asked Astrid.

"Yes, but that's what it's called, Giant Turkey on a Stick," said Apollo. "Don't worry—it's not a whole turkey!"

"Okay, one for me too, then," said Astrid. "So, the chubby bacon and turkey on a stick for the *salty* box. For *sour*, we should get lemonade,"

"Great idea! What should we get for *sweet*?" asked Mom.

Eliana pointed at the long lines of people in front of the cookie booth and cried, "Mar-tins!"

Mom looked over. "Oh yes! We have to get Martin's Biscuits. It wouldn't be the fair without those chocolate chip cookies!"

Apollo looked at the booth. He couldn't believe how many people were lined up. He counted twenty lines of people waiting to buy the cookies!

The lines were long and stretched so far back he couldn't see where they ended.

"The lines are too long! Can we get the cookies on our way home?" he asked.

Eliana shook her head. "Mar-tins Bis-kits now!"

Dad sighed. "Eliana and I will get in line for the chocolate chip cookies. The rest of you get turkey sticks, bacon, and lemonade."

"Then our scavenger hunt sheet will be done!" Astrid said.

"And our stomachs will be full!" Apollo said and rubbed his belly.

CHAPTER 5

Soo-per Surprise Prize

After they got all the food and drinks, Astrid and Apollo found an empty table for everyone to sit at. They ate their turkey sticks while Mom and Dad ate bacon strips. Mom had also bought a corn dog for Eliana.

"You can eat the cookies *after* the corn dog," Mom said to her.

Eliana frowned and bit into her corn dog.

"This turkey is good, but it would be even better with sticky rice," said Astrid.

"And pepper!" said Apollo.

"Oh, that would go great with the chubby bacon too," said Dad.

"Next time, I'll pack some spicy pepper sauce in my purse," Mom said.

Apollo and Dad laughed.

Astrid smiled. The warm cookies were spilling from their little paper basket onto the bench. She could smell the sweet cookies and see the melting chocolate chips oozing from them.

"Martin's Biscuits are the greatest," she said. "We can't come to the fair without eating them."

Apollo licked his lips. "I'm eating some as soon as I finish my drumstick!"

Eliana chewed her corn dog and said, "Soo-per."

"Your corn dog is super?" Dad asked her.

Eliana stood up. "Soo-per!" she repeated.

"That again? What is she saying?" Apollo asked.

"It's a mystery," said Astrid. She put her arm around Eliana. "Sorry we were busy playing the scavenger hunt game all day. But try and tell us. What is this super sippy thing you keep talking about?"

Eliana began pointing again. Dad picked her up. "Let's go for a walk, Gao Chee, and you can show me," he said to her.

After Dad and Eliana left, Astrid took out the scavenger hunt sheet. All nine boxes had words written inside them.

"We found everything here. We got *see, hear, touch, smell,* and *taste*," Astrid said.

"Excellent!" said Mom.

Apollo read what they had written down. "Sour lemonade, sweet Martin's Biscuits, and salty bacon and turkey sticks. Then we have beautiful butterflies, Hmong music, smelly barn smells, and wet stingrays."

"Don't forget the cold snow cones and hot corn on the cob," added Astrid.

Mom checked over the sheet too. "Great job! Now we just need to look for the X on the map to turn this in."

Apollo flipped the sheet to the back and studied the map. "It looks like we're close to it."

Astrid turned to see a table with teenagers holding the green papers. "Look, it's right there!"

"Let's go!" said Apollo.

"Now we'll find out what our surprise prize is!" said Astrid.

The twins stood up from the table just as Dad and Eliana were coming back.

"I figured out what Eliana's been wanting!" said Dad happily.

"Just a minute, Dad," said Astrid.

"We're going to get our prize!"

The family walked up to the scavenger hunt tables. Astrid handed in their sheet.

"Thank you!" said the same teenage girl from before. After she read it, she said, "Congratulations! Using your five senses, you found everything on your Family Fun Fair Day Scavenger Hunt. Now it's time for your prize."

She reached into an envelope and pulled out a long roll of tickets. "Here are twenty-five free tickets to use for the Super Slippery Slope!"

She pointed to the huge yellow slides behind them.

Apollo's eyes widened. Astrid's mouth dropped open.

Eliana clapped her hands and giggled. "See, see, see! Soo-per sip-puh-dee slow!"

"Amazing. We won exactly what Eliana has been asking for the whole day!" Dad said.

For the rest of the afternoon, Astrid, Apollo, Eliana, Mom, and Dad climbed up the long flight of stairs. Then they slid down the Super Slippery Slope slides. Over and over and over again. They laughed and screamed in delight every time.

- Hmong people first lived in southern China. Many of them moved to Southeast Asia in the 1800s. Some Hmong decided to stay in the country of Laos (pronounced *LAH-ohs*).

LAOS

- In the 1950s, a war called the Vietnam War started in Southeast Asia. The United States joined this war. They asked the Hmong in Laos to help them. When the U.S. lost the war, Hmong people had to leave Laos.

- After 1975, many Hmong came to the U.S. as refugees. Refugees are people who escape from their country to find a new, safe place to live. Today, Minnesota is home to around 80,000 Hmong.

- Many Hmong American families enjoy outdoor activities like camping, boating, and fishing.

bubble tea—a sweet dessert drink that comes in different flavors and has chewy black balls made of tapioca

fish sauce—a strong, salty sauce that is used as a seasoning for Hmong and other Southeast Asian dishes

pandan—a tropical plant used as a sweet flavoring in Southeast Asian cakes and desserts

pepper sauce—a very spicy sauce made with chopped Thai chili peppers, lime, and fish sauce. It is used as a dip for meat.

pork and green vegetable soup—pork and leafy green vegetables boiled in a broth. This is a typical dish that Hmong families eat at mealtime.

rice in water—a bowl or plate of rice with water added to it. Many Hmong children and elderly Hmong people like to eat rice this way.

spring roll—fresh vegetables, cooked rice noodles, and meat wrapped in soft rice paper. Spring rolls are different from egg rolls because they are not fried.

sticky rice—soft, sticky rice that kids like to smush into little balls and eat by hand. The rice is a light cream or purple color.

GLOSSARY

aquarium (ah-KWAIR-ee-um)—a place where fish and other water animals are kept

audience (AW-dee-uhnss)—people who watch or listen to a play, movie, or show

biscuit (BISS-kit)—a small doughy roll, or another word for a cookie

gondola (GAWN-duh-luh)—a passenger car suspended from cables that transports people above ground

grandstand (GRAND-stand)—a large stage or stadium

husk (HUSSK)—the outer layer, as around a cob of corn

inflatable (in-FLAY-tuh-buhl)—able to be blown up with air

international (in-ter-NASH-uh-nuhl)—involving more than one country

midway (MIDD-way)—the area of a fair or carnival with games or rides

scavenger hunt (SCAV-en-jer HUNT)—a game in which players need to find certain items

stingray (STING-ray)—a fish with a round, flat shape and a long tail

TALK ABOUT IT

1. Eliana is frustrated that her family doesn't understand what she's asking for. How do you think Eliana's family should have responded?

2. It's International Hmong Day at the fair. Astrid and Apollo's family watch performers sing and dance to traditional Hmong music. Have you ever attended a cultural celebration? Recall what you saw, heard, smelled, and tasted there.

WRITE IT DOWN

1. It's a yearly tradition for Astrid and Apollo's family to go to the state fair. Do you have a tradition in your family for something that happens only once a year? Write a paragraph about your tradition.

2. Astrid and Apollo's family have a great time at the fair—especially eating all the fun foods! Make a list of the foods their family eats in the story. Write an adjective (describing word) next to each food about how it tastes, or how you think it would taste.

3. Imagine that you are going to a fair. Draw a map of the fair and include all the things you think a fair should have—game booths, food stands, animals, rides? Then draw the route you'll take to each of the stops you'd like to make at the fair!

ABOUT THE AUTHOR

V.T. Bidania has been writing stories ever since she was five years old. She was born in Laos and grew up in St. Paul, Minnesota, right where Astrid and Apollo live! She has an MFA in creative writing from The New School and is a McKnight Writing Fellow. She lives outside of the Twin Cities and spends her free time reading all the books she can find, writing more stories, and playing with her family's sweet Morkie.

ABOUT THE ILLUSTRATOR

Evelt Yanait is a freelance children's digital artist from Barcelona, Spain, where she grew up drawing and reading wonderful illustrated books. After working as a journalist for an NGO for many years, she decided to focus on illustration, her true passion. She loves to learn, write, travel, and watch documentaries, discovering and capturing new lifestyles and stories whenever she can. She also does social work with children and youth, and she's currently earning a Social Education degree.